Unicorn Princesses

THE MOONBEAMS

The Unicorn Princesses series

Unicorn Princesses

THE MOONBEAMS

Emily Bliss

illustrated by Sydney Hanson

BLOOMSBURY
CHILDREN'S BOOKS
NEW YORK LONDON OXFORD NEW DELHI SYDNEY

BLOOMSBURY CHILDREN'S BOOKS
Bloomsbury Publishing Inc., part of Bloomsbury Publishing Plc
1385 Broadway, New York, NY 10018

BLOOMSBURY, BLOOMSBURY CHILDREN'S BOOKS, and the Diana logo
are trademarks of Bloomsbury Publishing Plc

First published in the United States of America in September 2020
by Bloomsbury Children's Books
www.bloomsbury.com

Text copyright © 2020 by Emily Bliss
Illustrations copyright © 2020 by Sydney Hanson

Bloomsbury books may be purchased for business or promotional use. For information on
bulk purchases please contact Macmillan Corporate and Premium Sales Department at
specialmarkets@macmillan.com

Library of Congress Cataloging-in-Publication Data
Names: Bliss, Emily, author. | Hanson, Sydney, illustrator.
Title: The Moonbeams / by Emily Bliss ; [illustrated by] Sydney Hanson.
Description: New York : Bloomsbury, 2020. | Series: Unicorn princesses ; 9 |
Summary: Unicorn princesses Sunbeam and Moon start a show choir, inviting everyone
in the enchanted Rainbow Realm to join, including human friend Cressida.
Identifiers: LCCN 2020021997 (print) | LCCN 2020021998 (e-book)
ISBN 978-1-5476-0483-8 (paperback) • ISBN 978-1-5476-0484-5 (v. 9 ; hardcover) •
ISBN 978-1-5476-0485-2 (v. 9 ; e-book)
Subjects: CYAC: Unicorns—Fiction. | Princesses—Fiction. | Magic—Fiction. |
Choirs (Music)—Fiction.
Classification: LCC PZ7.1.B633 Mo 2020 (print) | LCC PZ7.1.B633 (e-book)
DDC [Fic]—dc23
LC record available at https://lccn.loc.gov/2020021997
LC e-book record available at https://lccn.loc.gov/2020021998

Book design by Jessie Gang and John Candell
Typeset by Westchester Publishing Services
Printed and bound in the U.S.A. by Berryville Graphics Inc., Berryville, Virginia
2 4 6 8 10 9 7 5 3 1 (paperback)
2 4 6 8 10 9 7 5 3 1 (hardcover)

To find out more about our authors and books visit www.bloomsbury.com
and sign up for our newsletters.

For Phoenix and Lynx

Unicorn Princesses

THE MOONBEAMS

Chapter One

In the top tower of Spiral Palace, Ernest, a wizard-lizard, lay on his stomach, halfway under his bed. "It must be here somewhere," he muttered. "I know it is." He shoved aside his rock collection, a pile of crumpled pointy hats, a stack of dirty plates, a bicycle helmet, a full jar of oats, and a pair of white bunny slippers. "Found it!" Ernest cried, as he grabbed an orange book wedged under a unicycle, a typewriter, and a pair of teal galoshes.

He slid out from under the bed and stood up. His purple pointy hat sat sideways on his head, and dust covered his long nose. He sneezed three times and used his scaly green hands to brush off his face. Then he straightened his hat and laid the book down on his desk. In purple script, across the cover, was the title, *The Grainest Show on Earth: Spells for Turning Household Grains into Costumes, Props, and Performance Accessories.*

Ernest flipped to the table of contents and read the entries out loud as he slowly dragged a clawed finger down the page.

"'Couscous for Conjuring Tutus and Leotards.' Sounds like fun, but not today," Ernest said. "'Bewitching Wheat to Create Stages and Curtains.' No. 'Enchanting Rice for Ballet Slippers and Tap Shoes.' Maybe later. 'Turning Quinoa into Costumes.' Nope. 'Transforming Oats into Tickets.' Yes! That's the one. And it's on page 46."

Ernest flipped to page 46. He read over the spell four times, silently mouthing the words. Then, hopping with excitement, he said, "This is perfect! I even have oats—I just saw them!" He dived back under his bed and grabbed the jar of oats. He put it on his desk next to the spell book.

"Sunbeam and Moon will absolutely love this," Ernest said, rubbing his hands together. "And I'm sure I've got the spell memorized. No need to look again at the book."

He reached into his cloak pocket and pulled out his wand. He held it above the jar of oats and chanted, "Iggledy Figgledly Smiggledy Smo! Turn the Notes into Crickets for the Show!"

Ernest stared at the oats. He waited for light to swirl around the jar, or for the oats to vibrate and dance inside it. But instead, for several seconds, nothing happened. Ernest shrugged and muttered, "Maybe I ought to give it another go." He lifted his wand and opened his mouth. But before he could even say, "Iggledy," thunder rumbled and boomed. Ernest looked out his window just as black and yellow bolts of lightning tore through the sky and touched down in a glittering purple canyon in the distance.

"Oh dear, oh dear!" Ernest groaned. "I must have said the wrong thing. Again." He rolled his eyes and shook his head. He took a long deep breath. "This time, I'll read the spell as I cast it." He pushed his lips into a determined line. With his eyes fixed on page 46, he chanted, "Iggledy Figgledly Smiggledy Smo! Turn the Oats into Tickets for the Show!"

The oats glowed and flickered yellow and black. They spun and jiggled inside the jar. Then, with a flash of light, the jar of oats disappeared and in its place was a roll of yellow and black tickets.

"I did it!" Ernest exclaimed. He tore off a ticket and read out loud, "Admit One: The Moonbeams' First Concert."

Chapter Two

Cressida Jenkins opened the door of the red station wagon and slid out of the back seat. She grabbed her backpack—a glittery orange one, with rainbow straps, that said "Cressida" in gemstones across the outer compartment. "Thank you for driving me home, Ms. Blackburn," Cressida said to her friend Gillian's mother.

"Any time, Cressida," Ms. Blackburn said.

Cressida turned to Gillian. "See you in school tomorrow!" Cressida belted out as she extended her arms and spread her fingers so she had what their chorus teacher, Ms. Archibald, called "jazz hands."

Gillian threw back her head and laughed. Then she put jazz hands on either side of her face, fluttered her fingers, and sang, "Have a great afternoon."

Ms. Blackburn smiled. "You two girls are a riot," she said. "You have more fun than anyone I know. Especially when Eleanor is with you."

Cressida smiled. Gillian and Eleanor were her two best friends, and Ms. Blackburn was right—the three of them had enormous amounts of fun together.

"Thanks again for the ride," Cressida said, and she gently closed the station wagon door and took a step back. As Gillian and Cressida waved at each other, Ms. Blackburn drove away. When the station wagon had disappeared down a hill, Cressida turned around and ·skipped up her driveway, along her family's brick walkway, and through the front door. She danced into her house singing, "I'm home! I'm home! I'm home!" as she twirled and snapped her fingers.

"Hi sweetheart," her father called from the kitchen. "How was chorus practice?"

"Fantastic!" Cressida sang. She loved chorus practice. She loved it so much that she was always in an amazing mood for the rest of the afternoon.

"Wonderful! Marvelous!" her father sang back. She heard him chopping vegetables to make lasagna for dinner. Her mother was on a business trip, and so her father had taken the afternoon off from work.

Corey, Cressida's older brother, lay on his back on the couch with an open book propped against his bent legs. Cressida could see he was studying a two-page spread with pictures of crickets and grasshoppers. "Please go sing and dance somewhere else," Corey grumbled. But then he smiled and sang, "It's just that I'm trying to read in here!"

Cressida laughed. "Okay," she said, looking at his book. "But first tell me something about crickets."

Corey nodded. He loved learning and sharing facts about insects and animals. "Here's a good one," he said. He looked down at his book and read, "Crickets mainly chirp at night, and they're usually silent during the day. Crickets chirp by rubbing their wings together."

"Interesting," Cressida said. Then, with her jazz hands extended, she belted out, "Thanks for the facts!" before she skipped down the hallway to her bedroom. She closed her door, turned on her unicorn lamp, and laid her backpack on her unicorn bedspread. For a moment, Cressida smiled as she remembered everything that had happened at chorus practice that afternoon. Their teacher, Ms. Archibald, had taught them new choreography—that was the word for the ways they moved their arms and hands while they sang—and they had tried on their costumes: glittery red top hats with matching bow ties. One of the chorus room walls was covered in mirrors, and Cressida had loved watching all the chorus members singing and practicing their choreography in their hats and bow ties.

Cressida knew she needed to start her math homework. She even wanted to do it, because she was looking forward to figuring out the solutions to a new set of word problems. The trouble, though, was that doing her math homework meant sitting down at a desk. And right then, all the exhilaration and excitement of singing still sizzled through her, from the tips of her toes to the ends of her fingers. Sitting, even to do something she liked, felt completely impossible. Cressida bounded over to the center of her room, right in the middle of her unicorn rug. She decided she would jump up and down until she had gotten out enough energy that she could tolerate time at her desk.

Cressida counted her jumps out loud. And each time she jumped, her silver unicorn sneakers—which had pink, blinking lights—flashed. Just as she finished her twenty-third jump and was crouching down for the next, she heard a high, tinkling noise coming from her bedside table drawer. Cressida grinned from ear to ear. She fluttered her jazz hands. And she made her twenty-fourth jump a leap over to her bedside table. She opened the drawer and pulled out an old-fashioned key with a

crystal ball handle that was glowing bright pink and pulsing.

The key had been a gift from the unicorn princesses—eight unicorns with unique magic powers who ruled the Rainbow Realm, an enchanted world Cressida could travel to by pushing the key into a tiny hole at the base of an oak tree in the woods behind her house. Whenever the unicorns wanted to invite Cressida to the Rainbow Realm for a special occasion, they made the key glow bright pink and ring with a high tinkling noise.

A visit to the Rainbow Realm sounded like a perfect plan to Cressida. Not only would she be able to run and jump and play with unicorns instead of sitting at a desk, but time in the human world froze while she was in the Rainbow Realm. That meant she would still have time to do her homework before dinner once she returned.

As Cressida was about to run out of her room, she glanced down at her clothes. Her blue T-shirt was covered in stains from lunch: three large drips of chocolate milk, a glob of strawberry jam, a streak of guacamole, and a splatter of hummus. Luckily, her jeans looked just fine, apart from a hole in one knee—she thought of the tear as air conditioning for her legs when she was running on the playground. Cressida took off her dirty T-shirt and threw it in her hamper. She opened her shirt drawer and chose a bright yellow shirt with a black owl on the front. Now she was ready to visit Princess Sunbeam, Princess Flash, Princess Bloom, Princess Prism, Princess Breeze, Princess Moon, Princess Firefly, and Princess Feather.

Cressida shoved the key into her back pocket and raced down the hallway. In the living room, she sang, "I'm going for a quick walk in the woods."

"Just be back for dinner," her father sang from the kitchen.

Cressida sprinted out the back door and across her yard, into the woods behind her house. She jogged along the trail that led to the magic oak tree, skipping and twirling with excitement. When she reached the tree, she kneeled down and slid the key into a small hole. Suddenly, the forest began to spin, faster and faster, until everything was a blur of blue sky and green leaves. Then it went pitch black, and Cressida felt the exciting—and just a little bit frightening— sensation of falling through space.

After a few seconds, Cressida landed on something soft. At first, all she could see was a spinning swirl of pink, purple, and white. Then the room slowed to a stop, and Cressida knew exactly where she was: Spiral Palace, the unicorn princesses' horn-shaped home.

Chapter Three

In the front hall of Spiral Palace, light from the chandeliers shimmered and danced on the polished marble floors. Pink and purple curtains fluttered in the breeze. Large velvet armchairs and sofas sat near a row of silver troughs. Cressida looked around for Sunbeam, Flash, Bloom, Prism, Breeze, Moon, Firefly, and Feather, but they were nowhere to be seen. Just as Cressida was about to call out, "Hello?" she heard the sounds of singing.

The singing grew louder and louder, and for a few seconds, Cressida closed her eyes and listened. Two of the voices sounded so beautiful that goose bumps covered Cressida's arms and shivers shot up her spine. Most of the other voices were a little off-key, sometimes hitting the right notes and sometimes almost hitting them—that was how Cressida supposed she sounded when she sang. And two voices never hit the right notes at all. But every voice sounded full of exactly the same joy Cressida felt when she sang with her chorus.

Cressida opened her eyes as all eight unicorn princesses marched into the front hall, singing, swishing their tails, flicking their manes, and stomping their hooves. They sang for another minute, and as she watched, Cressida could see that Moon and Sunbeam were the two unicorns with the beautiful voices— Cressida figured that if they were in her school's chorus, Ms. Archibald would give them both solos. Bloom, Prism, Breeze, and Firefly's singing—like Cressida's— was sometimes a little off-key. But Flash and Feather hit so many wrong notes they sounded like they were singing a different song entirely.

When the unicorn princesses finished, Cressida jumped up and clapped, calling out, "Bravo! Bravo! That was amazing!"

Yellow Sunbeam, silver Flash, green Bloom, purple Prism, blue Breeze, black Moon, orange Firefly, and pink Feather all grinned. As they bent forward to bow, their gemstone necklaces shimmered in the light of the chandeliers.

When they stood back up, Sunbeam exclaimed, "My human girl is back! My human girl is back!" as she trotted in circles around Cressida.

"We're thrilled you're here," Moon said.

"Welcome!" Flash and Feather said at the same time.

Bloom and Breeze smiled at Cressida.

Firefly winked.

And Prism reared up and whinnied with excitement.

"I'm so glad to see all of you again," Cressida said. "And I loved hearing you sing."

"Thank you," Sunbeam said.

"Yes, thank you," Moon said. "Though we sound much better when we can read the notes from our sheet music while we sing."

"And when the raccoons are accompanying us on their instruments," Bloom said.

"And when the owls are hooting and the frogs are croaking," Firefly said.

"And when the cacti and the dunes are singing the harmony," Feather said. "They drown out all my wrong notes."

Flash laughed and nodded. "Exactly!" she said.

Cressida took a moment to imagine so many magical creatures singing together. "It sounds like you have an entire chorus," she said.

Moon and Sunbeam grinned proudly.

"Sunbeam and I started the first Rainbow Realm chorus just last week," Moon said.

"We call ourselves the Moonbeams," Sunbeam said.

"And we invited you because our first performance is this afternoon," Moon said.

"Ernest told me he even made tickets to pass out to all the creatures in the Rainbow Realm."

"So," Sunbeam and Moon said at exactly the same time, "would you like to come to our concert?"

Cressida's eyes widened. At that moment, a Rainbow Realm chorus concert sounded like the most exciting thing Cressida could imagine. "Absolutely," Cressida said, hopping from one foot to the other. "And guess what? I'm in a chorus, too! It's at my school, Pinewood Elementary."

"Really?" Sunbeam asked. "You like to sing?"

"I love to sing," Cressida said.

Sunbeam and Moon turned and looked at each other. Sunbeam raised her eyebrows, as if to ask her sister a silent question. Moon widened her eyes and nodded. Sunbeam nodded back. Then, the two unicorns faced Cressida. "The Moonbeams are made up of unicorns and creatures from the Glitter Canyon and the Night Forest," Sunbeam explained. "But we would be honored if you would be our special guest singer from the human world. Would you like to join us?"

Cressida's heart skipped a beat. "Yes," she said, clapping her hands, "that would be amazing."

"Fabulous," Sunbeam said.

"Terrific," Moon said. "We can figure

out what part you'll sing while we're getting ready for the concert."

"Speaking of getting ready," Sunbeam said, "we'd better do just that."

Moon nodded. She turned to Flash, Bloom, Prism, Breeze, Firefly, and Feather. "Good job practicing, Moonbeams," she said. "We'll meet you at the Glitter Canyon for our performance in two hours."

Flash and Feather nodded.

Bloom and Prism began to hum while Breeze and Firefly tapped their hooves to the beat.

"Are you ready to go?" Moon asked Cressida.

Cressida opened her mouth to say yes, but before she could make a sound, a nasal voice called out, "Wait! Don't go yet! Just a moment!" Cressida giggled.

Ernest burst into the room wearing his purple wizard's cloak, his pointy hat, and a pair of bunny slippers.

"I love those slippers," Cressida said.

"Thank you," Ernest said, holding one foot out and then the other so Cressida and the unicorns could admire the white furry ears and bright pink noses on Ernest's toes. "I found them under my bed. I'd completely forgotten my cousin Ignatius the Iguana sent them to me from the Reptile Realm."

"Do the iguanas wear bunny slippers in the Reptile Realm?" Flash asked, furrowing her brow.

"Sometimes," Feather said. "I saw the iguanas wearing them before bed on my last trip to the Reptile Realm."

Flash nodded and looked a little wistful,

as though she wished she could go on a trip.

"Guess what?" Ernest said, pulling a roll of yellow and black tickets from his pocket. "I made the tickets. And I did it on my first try. Well, almost on my first try. It was more like my second. But, um, anyway," Ernest said, clearing his throat. "I'm about to go give out tickets to all the creatures in the Rainbow Realm. And I'm going to do it wearing my bunny slippers."

Cressida giggled again.

"Thank you so much for making the tickets," Sunbeam said.

Moon nodded. "Yes, thank you."

"My pleasure," Ernest said. "Before I go, I have a magical surprise for Cressida.

I've been practicing this spell for most of the morning. I'm sure I can get it on my first try."

Cressida smiled and braced herself for a magical mishap.

Ernest dropped the roll of tickets back into his cloak pocket and pulled out his wand. He pointed it at Cressida, and as he waved it back and forth, he chanted, "Bubbly Snubbly Notily Snome! Make Magical High-Grow Foam!"

A comet of light zipped around the room in faster and faster circles. Then, with a bright flash, a thick carpet of sea-green foam covered the palace's marble floors. Right before Cressida's eyes, it began to grow. Ernest, Cressida, and the unicorns watched as the foam rose higher and higher, soon reaching their ankles and then their knees.

"Oh dear, oh dear," Ernest said, shaking his head. "This happened up in my room, too. It grew as high as my nose the first time, before I figured out how to get rid of it. The only good thing about it is it tastes like cherries. I figured that out by accident." Ernest blushed. Cressida laughed. She looked down and saw the foam was already touching her waist.

Ernest raised his wand and chanted, "Bubbly Fubbly Freebly Flee! Send the Foam off to the Sea! Singedy Songedy Trappedy Trome! Now Make a Magical Microphone!"

Light and wind swirled around Cressida. The foam disappeared, and she felt something in her hand. She looked down, and there was a purple microphone.

"Thank you, Ernest," Cressida said.

"No problem," Ernest said. "I thought it might come in handy at the concert. And now I really must be going. I have tickets to give away." He spun around in his bunny slippers and skipped down the hall, calling out, "Tickets! Tickets! Come get your tickets!"

Cressida and the unicorns all looked at each other and smiled.

"Now we really do need to go get ready," Sunbeam said.

"And our first stop is the Night Forest,"

Moon said. "I promised the owl family we'd listen to them practice their hooting one last time before the concert."

"That sounds great!" Cressida said, and she pushed the microphone into her jeans pocket.

"I even have your magic glasses from your last visit to the Night Forest," Moon said, nodding toward a large, purple armchair. Cressida looked, and sure enough, in the center of the velvet cushion sat a pair of pink glasses dotted with opals. Ernest had made them for Cressida on her last visit to the Night Forest so she would be able to see in the dark. Cressida skipped over to the armchair, picked up the glasses, and slid them into her pocket next to the microphone.

Moon knelt in front of Cressida. "Climb on up," she said. "I can't wait to introduce you to the owls."

"I can't wait, either," Cressida said, swinging her leg over Moon's back.

Moon galloped out the front door of the palace with Sunbeam right behind her.

Chapter Four

Moon and Sunbeam trotted side by side along the clear stones that led from Spiral Palace into the surrounding forest. Cressida, sitting on Moon's back and gripping the unicorn's shiny black mane, turned to admire the unicorn princesses' pearly, horn-shaped castle. And then she giggled: green foam was dripping out the window of the palace's top turret.

Cressida faced forward again as Moon and Sunbeam veered onto a path that wound through a thick pine forest.

"I just can't wait for the concert this afternoon," Sunbeam said, her hooves crunching on the pinecones that littered the forest floor. "It's going to be amazing. And we're thrilled you'll be joining us."

"I'm really excited too," Cressida said.

"The Moonbeams have been practicing day and night," Moon said.

"I don't think I've ever worked this hard at anything," Sunbeam said, laughing. "I've hardly even taken a break from practicing to sunbathe or roll in the Glitter Canyon's purple clover."

"I'm even more excited for our concert than I was for the Starlight Ball," Moon said. "And the Starlight Ball is my favorite day of the year."

"You sounded like you were having so much fun singing together," Cressida said.

"We were," Sunbeam said. She paused for a moment. And then she added, "I think my favorite thing about the Moonbeams is we decided not to hold any auditions."

"We agreed to ask all our sisters to join, regardless of how well any of them sing," Moon said. "We didn't want anyone to feel excluded. The point of the Moonbeams is to have fun together."

Moon and Sunbeam turned onto a narrow path that passed through groves of cherry and maple trees before following a thick hedge with thorny vines and yellow, moon-shaped flowers. The unicorns stopped in front of an opening in the hedge.

"Why don't you put on your glasses now?" Moon said.

Cressida fished the glasses from her pocket and put them on as Moon and Sunbeam leaped through the opening. Cressida closed her eyes. When she opened them, she was in the Night Forest. A pale yellow moon hung in the sky amid thousands of tiny silver stars. Right in front of her was the pond she remembered from her last visit, and for a few seconds she watched the giant blue frogs, perched on lily pads, as their throats ballooned out. A line of skunks—two grown-ups and eight babies—marched through the meadow on the far side of the pond. Cressida turned and looked at the edge of the forest. The last time she'd visited, white and silver owls, all with glowing yellow eyes, had winked at her in the tree branches. But now the owls were gone.

"I love the Night Forest," Cressida whispered.

"Thank you," Moon said, kneeling down. Cressida slid off her back onto a spongy carpet of green moss.

"This way to the owls' birdhouse," Moon said. Cressida grinned and felt her heart race with excitement. She couldn't wait to meet the owls and see their home.

Sunbeam, Moon, and Cressida followed a path around the pond and into the woods. When the forest floor began to grow bumpy with roots, Moon stopped in front of a pine tree.

"The owls' birdhouse is at the top of this tree," Moon explained. Then, she smiled mysteriously at Sunbeam and Cressida. "At the count of the three, close your eyes and hoot like an owl four times."

Sunbeam and Cressida looked at each other. Sunbeam shrugged. Cressida grinned and shrugged back.

"One," Moon began. "Two. Three."

Moon, Sunbeam, and Cressida shut their eyes and called out, "Hoo! Hoo! Hoo! Hoo!"

Cressida heard a rustling noise, like leafy branches rubbing against each other in the wind. Then there was the gentle thud of something landing on the ground in front of them.

"Now you can look," Moon said.

Cressida opened her eyes. There, in front of their feet and hooves, was a shallow bowl made of branches, twigs, leaves, string, yarn, and straw. It looked, Cressida thought, like a nest for a bird the size of two unicorns. "This," Moon explained, "is the nestivator. It's called that because it looks like a nest, but it's an elevator."

"I love the word 'nestivator,'" Cressida said, giggling.

Moon jumped into the nestivator and Sunbeam and Cressida climbed in beside her.

Moon cleared her throat and said in a loud voice, "Nestivator, please take us to the owls' birdhouse."

The nestivator glided forward, and Cressida put one hand on Sunbeam and one hand on Moon to steady herself. When the nestivator was a few feet away from the tree, it began to slowly rise, floating in spirals first around the bare brown trunk and then around thick masses of branches covered in green pine needles and pinecones. After a few minutes, the nestivator slowed down and stopped at the top of the tree. Right there, in front of Cressida, Moon, and Sunbeam, was a giant ball made of twigs, pine needles, feathers, string, leaves, vines, moss, and straw. At the bottom was a doorway with pinecones, strung like beads, hanging over it.

Moon swished her tail and said, "Follow me!" before she bounded off the nestivator and into the birdhouse.

"You can go next," Sunbeam said. "You

look even more excited than I am. And believe me, I'm excited!"

Cressida walked carefully to the edge of the nestivator—they were high off the ground, and she didn't want to fall—and took a giant step into the birdhouse. She felt Sunbeam following right behind her.

Inside, Cressida found a room unlike any other she'd ever seen. A sprawling chandelier made of acorns and pine needles hung from the ceiling. An owl-shaped rug, made of lily pads and ferns woven together, covered the floor. Perches made of gnarled wood jutted out from the walls. Across the room from the door was one large nest and two triple bunk nests—owl bunk beds that were each three nests high.

Sitting in a circle on the rug were eight silver owls—two grown-ups and six tiny chicks. They all had enormous, glowing, yellow eyes that were staring right at Cressida.

Chapter Five

"Cressida," Moon said, "it is my pleasure to introduce you to the owl family. Meet Opal and Otto." Moon nodded at the grown-up owls. "Opal and Otto, this is Cressida. She's going to be a special guest singer at our performance today."

"We're thrilled to meet you," Otto said.

"Yes. We've heard all about you," Opal said, nodding.

"It's wonderful to meet you, too," Cressida said.

The owl chicks began to hoot and hop and flap their wings.

Opal laughed. "Cressida, meet our children: Oliver, Owen, Orion, Odetta, Olivia, and Orly."

The six owl chicks hooted even louder and hopped up and down.

"Hello," Cressida said, kneeling down next to the chicks. "I'm glad to meet you!"

"We're glad to meet you, too," Orion said, doing a somersault.

"Yes," agreed Odetta, flapping her wings so she lifted a few inches off the floor.

"We've been hoping you'd come," Orly said, jumping onto Cressida's lap.

"We've never seen a human before," Owen said, pushing his face up against Cressida's, so his beak touched her nose.

Cressida laughed. "And I've never met owl chicks before," she said.

The chicks began to hop and hoot, and soon they were running in circles around the birdhouse.

"Oh my," Opal said, raising her eyebrows. Then, she called out, "Listening ears! Listening ears, little owls!"

Cressida smiled. Owl parents sounded a lot like human parents.

"Little owls," Otto said, "now is the time to line up to show Princess Moon and

Princess Sunbeam how much we've practiced our hooting for the concert."

The owl chicks quieted down. They were lining up across the rug when Orion whispered something to his brothers and sisters. Soon the owl chicks were huddled in a tight circle, whispering and hopping with excitement. After a few seconds, Olivia ran over to Otto and whispered in his ear. He chuckled and said, "Oh sure, why not?"

"Hooray! Hooray!" the owl chicks hooted. Then they hopped in circles and flapped their wings before they rushed up to Cressida.

"We have a question for you," Orly said,

jumping on Cressida's silver unicorn sneakers.

"Yes," Owen said, before he did three somersaults.

"We're wondering," Odetta said, doing a back flip.

"If you might hoot with us," Orion finished, twirling around on one talon.

"Hoot with us! Hoot with us!" the owl chicks all cried out at once.

"Please!" Odetta said.

Then, all the owl chicks called out, "Please! Please! Please! Please!"

Cressida giggled. "Right now?" she asked.

"Yes! Yes! Yes! Yes!" the chicks called

out, flapping their wings and somersaulting.

Cressida laughed even harder. Even though she wasn't an owl and had very little practice hooting, she thought joining the owl chicks for their practice session sounded like a lot of fun.

Cressida looked at Oliver, Owen, Orion, Odetta, Olivia, and Orly and said, "I'd love to join you!"

The owls chicks began sprinting in circles around the birdhouse, hooting so loudly Cressida covered her ears with her hands.

"They're just a little excited you're here," Opal said to Cressida, and she winked one of her enormous yellow eyes.

Then she called out, "Oliver, Owen, Orion, Odetta, Olivia, and Orly! Who has their listening ears on?"

The owl chicks kept hooting and running.

Opal and Otto flapped their wings to make a loud clapping noise.

The owl chicks still kept hooting and running.

Opal and Otto looked at each other and shook their heads.

Then Moon belted out, in her beautiful soprano voice, "Listening ears, little owls!"

The owls chicks finally stopped.

"Please line up with Cressida now," Otto said.

The owl chicks rushed over to Cressida.

Oliver, Orly, and Orion lined up on her right side, and Odetta, Olivia, and Owen lined up on her left.

"All you have to do is hoot to the beat," Olivia explained to Cressida.

"It's pretty easy," Orion said.

"And if you make a mistake, don't worry about it. Just keep going," Orly said.

"We don't have our sheet music, so let's just improvise for now. Don't worry about hooting the right notes," Olivia said.

"That sounds great," Cressida said.

"We'll begin at the count of three," Otto said. "One. Two. Three."

Opal began to clap her wings to a steady beat. For the first four claps, the owl chicks silently nodded their heads to the beat. And then they started to hoot.

Cressida listened, grinning with delight. And then she closed her eyes. She pretended she was an owl, with talons and tufted feathers that looked like ears. And then she joined in, calling out, "Hoo! Hoo! Hoo! Hoo! Hoo!"

After a few more seconds, when she

had nearly convinced herself she had wings and a beak, she opened her eyes. Oliver, Owen, Orion, Odetta, Olivia, and Orly were all hooting with wide, excited eyes. Cressida hooted with even more enthusiasm.

Soon, Cressida heard a voice singing, "Sha la la la la la!" She looked across the birdhouse to see it was Sunbeam. Moon smiled and then joined in harmony. Cressida, the owl family, Moon, and Sunbeam all hooted and sang for several more minutes. And then, Opal loudly clapped her wings three times, and everyone was silent. After a few seconds, Cressida, Moon, Sunbeam, and all the owls clapped.

"That was absolutely amazing," Moon

said. "I can really tell you've been working hard."

Sunbeam nodded. "All your practicing has paid off."

"And," Opal said, winking, "Cressida is a natural owl."

Otto nodded. "She hoots just as well as we do."

Orly turned to Cressida and asked, "Will you hoot with us in the concert this afternoon?"

The owl chicks began to hop and flap their wings. "Please! Please! Please!" they shouted.

Cressida smiled at the owl chicks. "Yes," she said, "I would love to hoot with you in the concert this afternoon."

The owl chicks began to hoot and jump. But before they could start running in circles, Opal called out, "Listening ears, little owls! It's time to take a nap so you're well rested for the concert. Please say goodbye to Princess Moon, Princess Sunbeam, and Cressida and hop over to your bunk nests."

"Goodbye! Goodbye! See you soon!" Oliver, Owen, Orion, Odetta, Olivia, and Orly called out. They raced across the birdhouse toward the bunk nests, and each owl chick leaped into a nest. They tucked their faces under their wings. In a matter of seconds, they were asleep, and Cressida could hear a soft noise that sounded like a cross between snoring and hooting.

Opal and Otto looked at the sleeping owl chicks and smiled at each other.

Then, Otto whispered, "If you don't mind, please try not to wake up the chicks as you leave."

"Of course," Moon whispered back.

And then, on the tips of their hooves, Sunbeam and Moon walked across the bird-house and disappeared through the strings of pinecone beads.

Cressida smiled at the owl chicks. "Thank you so much for including me," she whispered to Opal and Otto.

"Any time," Otto whispered.

"See you at the concert," Opal whispered.

Cressida turned and followed Sunbeam and Moon. Outside the birdhouse, she found the unicorns waiting on the nestivator. She stepped onto it and put one hand on each unicorn's back.

"Please take us back down," Moon said.

The nestivator spiraled down the tree and landed gently on the ground.

"Our next stop is the Glitter Canyon," Sunbeam said, swishing her tail. She kneeled down, looked at Cressida, and said, "Climb on up."

Cressida swung a leg over Sunbeam's back and held on to the unicorn's soft yellow mane.

Sunbeam reared up and sang out, "This way to the Glitter Canyon!" before she and

Moon galloped back through the forest, around the pond, and out the opening in the hedge. Cressida took off her magic glasses and slid them back into her pocket. She couldn't wait to visit the Glitter Canyon again.

Chapter Six

Moon and Sunbeam ran side by
side until they took a sharp
right turn onto a trail that led
down a steep hill. As they descended, Cressida, riding on Sunbeam's back, noticed
it was getting warmer and warmer, and she
was glad her jeans had a hole in the knee.

Moon and Sunbeam turned left onto a

narrow, sandy path. And then, after a few minutes, they stopped right on the edge of a giant sparkling purple canyon.

"Welcome back to the Glitter Canyon," Sunbeam said, and she kneeled so Cressida could slide off her back.

The Glitter Canyon was just as beautiful as Cressida remembered. Glittery purple sand sparkled everywhere. Plum-colored rocks, clumps of lavender grass, and clusters of violets covered the canyon walls. Scattered along the trails that led to the bottom of the canyon were pebbles that reminded Cressida of silvery grapes.

Moon smiled and closed her eyes. "I have to admit that even I love the feeling of the sun on my shoulders," she said. "Especially after spending time in the Night Forest."

Cressida nodded. She, too, loved the feeling of the sun on her face and shoulders.

"I wish we could spend a few hours rolling around in the purple clover," Sunbeam said, "but we'd better hike down to the base of the canyon and get ready. The raccoons will be here soon to start warming up their instruments, and the cacti and the dunes had hoped to fit in one more practice session."

"Plus, Otto and Opal wanted to bring the owl chicks early so they could have fun rolling down the dunes before the concert," Moon said.

Cressida couldn't help but giggle at the image of Oliver, Owen, Orion, Odetta, Olivia, and Orly tumbling down Danny, Denise, Darryl, Doris, Dave, and Devin— the six purple sand dunes she had met on her first visit to the Glitter Canyon.

Sunbeam, Moon, and Cressida hiked together to the bottom of the canyon. When they came to a stretch of glittery purple sand, Sunbeam said, "The cacti and the dunes are waiting for us right up here."

Sure enough, just ahead, Cressida saw several rows of stone benches lined up in front of a purple stage made of wood and stone. A yellow banner, mounted across the front of the stage, read, "THE MOONBEAMS" in black block letters. Six sand dunes and four flowering cacti stood on one side of the stage, their eyes wide with worry and their mouths bent in frowns. Scattered all over the stage were sheets of paper and music stands that looked as though they had toppled over.

"Why is the sheet music all over the place?" Sunbeam asked, sounding nervous. "And what on earth happened to the music stands?"

"That's awfully strange," Moon said. "This morning, we left the music stands set up for the concert and the sheet music in a neat stack with the cacti."

Sunbeam grimaced and galloped ahead. She leaped onto the stage and lowered her head to examine one of the pieces of paper. She looked at another. And then another. Then she turned, jumped off the stage, and galloped back to Moon and Cressida. Tears streamed down her cheeks.

"What's wrong?" Moon asked. "Is it just that the wind made a mess? Cressida has hands. I'm sure she can quickly pick up the stands and organize the sheet music."

"The mess is the least of our worries," Sunbeam said. "All the notes are missing."

"The notes are missing?" Moon asked, sounding confused.

"Yes," Sunbeam said. "Come look."

Moon and Cressida rushed after Sunbeam to the scattered sheet music. Up on the stage, Cressida kneeled down and picked up a paper that said, "Raccoons' Part," across the top. She saw the black horizontal lines that formed the staff for the treble clef—those were the high sounds—and the bass clef—the low sounds.

But just as Sunbeam said, the notes—the black dots on the lines that told singers what to sing and musicians what to play—were gone!

Cressida picked up another paper that said "Frogs' Part" across the top. There were no notes. She picked up a paper that said "Unicorns' Part" across the top. No notes. There were also no notes on the pages that said "Dunes' Part," "Cacti's Part," and "Owls' Part."

Moon furrowed her brow and bit her lip. After a few seconds, she said, "What will we do? I don't think we can hold the concert without our sheet music. I haven't memorized my part. And I don't think anyone else has, either."

Sunbeam shook her head. "Without the notes, the raccoons won't know what to play, and the unicorns, the cacti, and the dunes won't know what to sing."

"The frogs won't know what notes to croak and the owls won't know what notes to hoot," Moon said.

Sunbeam and Moon looked at each other with panicked faces.

"The whole concert is falling apart," Sunbeam said.

"We'll have to cancel it," Moon whispered. "We have no choice." Her eyes filled with tears.

Cressida looked at her unicorn friends. She could see how disappointed they felt. She felt disappointed, too—she had been even more excited to hoot with the Moonbeams than she was to sing with the Pinewood

74

Elementary School Chorus. She took a deep breath. "Before we cancel the concert," Cressida said, "let's see if we can figure out what happened to the notes. Maybe there's a way to put them back on the sheet music."

"It's worth a try," Moon said.

Sunbeam nodded. "Good idea," she said.

Cressida looked over at the dunes. Danny, Denise, Darryl, Doris, Dave, and Devin stared at her with worried faces. Then she looked at the cacti. Corrine, Claude, Carl, and Callie—who Cressida had met on her last visit to the Glitter Canyon—frowned and stared at the ground.

Cressida walked across the stage so she was standing next to them. "Hello," she said.

"Hello," the cacti and the dunes said, their voices sad and low.

"Sorry to sound so glum," Danny said.

"We're glad to see you," Doris added.

"Really, we are," Carl said.

"It's just that the sheet music is ruined," Corrine said.

"And we were excited for the concert," Callie said.

"The best day ever is turning into the worst," Devin finished.

"I completely understand you feel sad and disappointed," Cressida said. "I want to try to find the missing notes so we don't have to cancel the concert. Do you know what happened to them?"

Callie nodded. "I was holding the sheet music like this," she explained, bending her arms across her body.

"And then, it was strangest thing," Claude said.

"Yes," Carl said, "there was a lot of wind. Sort of like a small tornado."

"It swirled and swirled," Danny said. "It knocked over all the music stands."

"And then there was thunder and lightning," Doris explained.

"The sheet music scattered all over the stage," Denise said.

"But the weirdest part," Callie said,

"was that the notes turned into crickets and sprang off the pages."

The four cacti and the six dunes nodded.

"Crickets?" Moon, Sunbeam, and Cressida all said at once.

"Crickets," Corrine, Claude, Carl, Callie, Danny, Denise, Darryl, Doris, Dave, and Devin replied.

"Interesting," Cressida said.

"They hopped right on top of us," Denise said.

"It tickled," Darryl added, chortling.

"There were hundreds of them," Dave said. "I've never seen so many crickets."

"Do you know where they are now?" Cressida asked.

"No idea," Doris said.

"All we know is they're not here any more," Callie added, and the other cacti nodded.

Cressida heard Sunbeam sniffle.

Moon whispered, "How in the world are we going to find a few hundred crickets? They're tiny. They could be anywhere!"

Cressida closed her eyes and tried to come up with a plan. It was hard to think clearly and creatively with four cacti, six dunes, and two unicorns staring at her. But then, suddenly, she remembered the fact Corey had shared with her earlier that afternoon: crickets were mostly silent during the day, but they chirped at night.

"I have an idea to find the crickets!" Cressida said, jumping from one foot to the other. "Moon, can you make the Glitter Canyon pitch black?"

"Sure," Moon said, sounding confused, "though I think it's usually even harder to find anything in the dark. Especially something as small as a bug."

"I don't know if my idea will work," Cressida said. "But let's just try it."

Moon shrugged and nodded. The opal on her yellow ribbon necklace shimmered, and sparkling light poured from her horn. Suddenly, the Glitter Canyon was pitch black.

"How on earth will this help us?" Sunbeam said.

"Let's all just listen for a few seconds and see what happens," Cressida said.

"Listen for what?" Sunbeam asked.

But before Cressida could respond, they heard the sound of chirping.

Chapter Seven

"The crickets!" Sunbeam said, trotting in an excited circle. "I hear them!"

"Follow that sound!" Moon said, rearing up and whinnying.

Cressida pulled her magic glasses from her pocket and put them on. She kneeled down and gathered all the pages of noteless sheet music into a neat stack and tucked it under her arm. Then she, Sunbeam, and Moon jumped off the stage and began to run toward the chirping. They rushed along a stretch of sand, around patches of wildflowers, and behind a cluster of giant, plum-colored rocks. That's when Cressida saw, right before her eyes, hundreds of chirping crickets with bubbles floating up from their wings.

For a few seconds, Cressida, Moon, and Sunbeam watched and listened. As the crickets chirped and chirped, more and more bubbles rose up into the air. And then, suddenly, Cressida heard something familiar in the chirping, though she couldn't put her finger on exactly what it was.

Moon whispered, "When they started,

the crickets were chirping the frogs' part in our concert. Now they're chirping the unicorns' part."

Cressida sucked in her breath. That was it! The crickets were chirping the same song she'd heard the unicorns singing when she arrived at Spiral Palace.

Sunbeam nodded. They listened for a few more seconds, and she added, "Now they're chirping the raccoons' part."

For a moment, Sunbeam and Moon looked excited. But then Moon's face fell. "It's great that we found the crickets. But what do we do now?" she asked. "We can't exactly put them on our sheet music."

Sunbeam sighed. "This is still a complete disaster," she said.

Just then, a bubble floated over to Sunbeam and landed on her nose. For a moment, it quivered. And then it popped. To Cressida's surprise, on the tip of Sunbeam's nose, right where the bubble had been, was a black dot with a straight tail.

"What is that?" Sunbeam asked, crossing her eyes to look at it. She scrunched up her nose.

"I think," Cressida said, feeling excited, "it's a note!"

Sunbeam and Moon looked at each other.

"You mean the notes are trapped in the bubbles?" Sunbeam asked.

"Maybe," Cressida said. "Let me check to be sure." She walked closer to the crickets. A bubble floated up toward her face. She poked it with her index finger. The bubble popped, and a note appeared on her fingernail. She poked another bubble, this time with her pinky finger. Again, a note appeared on her fingernail. Cressida popped bubbles with her thumb, her middle finger, and her ring finger so she had a note on each fingernail. Then, she skipped over to Sunbeam and Moon. "There are definitely notes inside the bubbles," she said, and she held up her hand so the unicorns could see her decorated fingernails.

Moon smiled, but her eyes were still dark with worry. "That's good news," she said slowly, "but how will we get them back on the sheet music?"

Sunbeam bit her lip. "I'm thinking and thinking, but I don't have any ideas."

"I'm not ready to give up yet," Cressida said. For a few seconds, she listened to the chirping and watched the bubbles lifting up into the air and vanishing into the pitch black canyon. "I'm going to try something," she said slowly. She put the stack of sheet music down in the sand and grabbed just the top page, which said, "Unicorns' Part." She walked as close as she could get to the crickets without accidentally stepping on one. Bubbles floated all around her, and with one hand she held the paper right under a bubble drifting straight for her nose. With the other hand, she popped the bubble quickly, pulling her finger back as soon as it burst.

This time, instead of landing on her fingernail, the note fluttered down to the page of sheet music and settled onto the black horizontal lines. Cressida popped five more bubbles in exactly the same way. Then, she ran back to Moon and Sunbeam and held the paper so they could see it. "Are these six notes in the right places?" she asked.

The unicorns studied the page for a few seconds, humming softly together.

"Yes!" Sunbeam said, rearing up and

dancing in a circle. "Those are the first six notes of our part."

"Good work," Moon said, grinning. Then she paused. "But how can we pop enough bubbles before the concert? There are hundred of notes we still need to get back on the sheet music."

Sunbeam held up a golden hoof and frowned. "And Moon and I won't be much help since we don't have fingers."

Cressida nodded. And then she jumped up and down. "I know what to do!" she said. "Moon, would it be possible to go get the owl family?"

"Yes," Moon said. "I bet they're already in the Glitter Canyon."

Moon galloped back toward the stage.

After a few minutes, she returned with Otto and Opal, who were pushing two triple strollers that had nests instead of seats. Inside one sat Oliver, Orly, and Odetta. And inside the other stroller sat Owen, Orion, and Olivia. As soon as the owl chicks saw Cressida, they leaped from the strollers and rushed over to her.

Cressida kneeled down so she could look right at the owl chicks. "I have a very important job for you. Would you like to help us save the Moonbeams concert?"

"Yes! Yes! Yes!" Oliver, Owen, Orion, Odetta, Olivia, and Orly hooted.

"What I'm going to need you to do— " Cressida began, but the owl chicks were so loud and excited they couldn't hear her.

Cressida smiled. And then she said, "Listening ears! Listening ears, little owls!"

The owl chicks quieted down, though Orion and Odetta kept hopping. And Orly started flapping her wings. Cressida decided she had better tell them what to do quickly, before they all started hooting again.

"Good listening," Cressida said. "I'm going to put these pages down on the ground," she said, grabbing the stack of sheet music and lining up the pages on the sandy canyon floor, right next to the crickets. The owl chicks began to hoot again. "Listening ears!" Cressida called out. "What I need you to do is to pop all the bubbles you see, as fast as you can."

"Bubbles! Bubbles! Bubbles!" Oliver, Owen, Orion, Odetta, Olivia, and Orly hooted, hopping and flapping their wings and doing somersaults in the air.

And then, in a frenzy of jumping, flipping, and pecking, they popped the bubbles so quickly that all Cressida could see was a blur of silver feathers. Cressida heard the crickets chirp what she remembered Moon and Sunbeam had said were the frogs' part, the owls' part, the raccoons' part, the dunes' part, the cacti's part, and the unicorns' part. Right before her eyes, the sheet music filled up with notes.

"I think that's all of it," Sunbeam said after several minutes of the owl chicks' bubble popping.

Moon looked down at the sheet music. "Yes," she said, grinning and then rearing up with joy. "You saved the Moonbeams' concert! Thank you, Cressida!"

"Yes! Thank you!" Sunbeam said, and she danced in a circle.

Cressida quickly picked up the sheet music from the ground and put it in a neat stack.

"Thank you so much for your help, little owls!" But they were having so much fun jumping, popping bubbles, and watching the notes fall down onto the glittery sand that they didn't hear her.

Chapter Eight

"Sunbeam, I think you can go ahead and bring back the sunlight," Cressida said.

Sunbeam nodded. "I think you're right!" Her yellow sapphire shimmered. Golden light poured from her horn. And suddenly, the sun was out again in the Glitter Canyon.

Cressida took off her glasses and put

them back in her pocket. The crickets fell silent, and bubbles stopped floating from their wings. The owl chicks looked for more bubbles, and when they didn't see any, to Cressida's surprise, they all began to yawn and rub their eyes with their wings. With fluttering eyelids, they staggered over to the triple strollers, hopped into the nests, tucked their heads under their wings, and fell asleep.

Otto and Opal laughed. "I think popping bubbles completely exhausted them," Opal said.

"This is their fourth nap today," Otto said. "I'm sure it will be quick and they'll wake up in time for the concert."

Cressida giggled at the owl chicks, who

had begun to hoot-snore. Then she looked down at the sheet music. In the sunlight, she saw that sandy purple owl footprints covered the pages. She smiled and brushed them off. "I think we can go get ready for the concert now," she said.

Sunbeam, Moon, and Cressida hurried back to the stage. Opal and Otto, each pushing a stroller of sleeping owl chicks, followed right behind them. They found the dunes and the cacti looking worriedly at each other. A circle of Night Forest frogs sat on the stage, anxiously ballooning out their throats. Next to them, the raccoons stood with their instruments— a flarpophone, a quadruple-duple-banji-nano, a trumpledumpledordion, and an octogoloctohorn—swishing their tails. And the other six unicorn princesses—Flash, Bloom, Prism, Breeze, Firefly, and Feather— were waiting, humming to themselves, and nervously tapping their hooves against the wooden stage floor. Opal and Otto lifted the strollers onto the stage and parked them next to the frogs.

"The cacti and the dunes told us what happened," Firefly said. "Were you able to find the notes?"

Moon nodded. "Yes. Cressida saved the Moonbeams' concert!"

"I had a feeling she would," Feather said, winking at Cressida.

"What a relief," said Roland and Renee, two of the raccoons Cressida had met on her very first visit to the Night Forest. The other two raccoons, Ringo and Rita, began to pick up the music stands from the stage and set them up in front of the dunes, the cacti, the frogs, the unicorns, and the owls.

As Cressida put the sheet music on the stands, she looked up to see more creatures than she could count finding seats in the rows of benches in front of the stage. There were foxes, rabbits, gnomes, dragons, mini-dragons, rainbow cats, fairies, snails, skunks, opossums, and phoenixes, all holding yellow and black tickets. They looked expectantly at the Moonbeams.

"We almost forgot our hats," Moon said suddenly.

"Don't worry," Darryl said. "The

raccoons brought them from the Night Forest and left them right here on my head." The dune looked upward at several stacks of black glittery top hats, in all different sizes, decorated with golden suns and moons.

"Cressida, since you have hands, might you help us with our costumes?" Breeze asked.

"Absolutely," Cressida said. She walked over to Darryl and picked up the hats. She put the smallest ones on the frogs and on the owl chicks, who had just woken up, hopped out of their strollers, and taken their places in a line in front of their parents. She put the medium-size hats on Opal, Otto, the raccoons, the cacti, and the unicorns. And she put the biggest hats on the dunes. Then, to her surprise, she saw one more hat sitting on a rock next to the cacti. Cressida jumped off the stage, walked over to it, and picked it up. To her delight and surprise, it had a tag on it that said, "Dear Cressida, Here is a hat, just for you! Thank you for saving the Moonbeams' concert. Love, Ernest."

Cressida smiled. She put the hat on her head. And then she stepped back onto the stage, ran over to the owls, and got in line with them.

"Are we ready?" Sunbeam asked, looking at the Moonbeams.

"Yes!" called out the raccoons, the frogs,

the owls, the dunes, the cacti, the unicorn princesses, and, of course, Cressida.

"Fantastic," Moon said. Then, she looked at the audience and smiled. "Welcome to the Moonbeams' very first concert," she said. "We're so pleased you're here." Even though Moon was using her loudest voice, the Glitter Canyon was so big that the audience couldn't hear her.

Moon looked worriedly at Sunbeam. "I don't think anyone can hear me," she whispered.

"Uh oh," Sunbeam said.

And that's when Cressida remembered the gift from Ernest. "Just a second," Cressida said. "Don't panic yet."

She pulled the purple microphone

from her pocket and put it in the center of all the Moonbeams. The microphone shimmered.

Cressida cleared her throat and said, "Testing, testing. One. Two. Three." Her voice boomed and echoed against the canyon walls, as giant, ribbon-like rainbows sprayed from the top of the microphone.

"Yet again, Cressida saves the day," Prism said. "And I love those rainbows!"

Moon and Sunbeam smiled at each other and nodded. The two unicorns counted, "One and a two and a one, two, three, four."

The raccoons began to play, and the sounds of their instruments filled the canyon as even more rainbows shot from the

microphone. Soon, the frogs croaked. The dunes began to sing, "Doo, doo, doo, doo." The cacti sang, "Sha la la la la." The owls and Cressida hooted to the beat. And the unicorn princesses sang the song Cressida had heard them practicing in the palace.

As the Moonbeams sang song after song, the audience clapped to the beat, and rainbows filled the sky. When the concert ended, the audience cheered and clapped as the unicorns stepped forward and bowed. The Rainbow Realm creatures kept clapping as the dunes flattened themselves to bow and the cacti tilted forward. The frogs and the raccoons bowed. And finally, Cressida and the entire owl family stepped forward to bow.

When the audience finished clapping and yelling, "Bravo! Bravo!" Cressida smiled and took a long, deep breath. Hooting with the owls in the Moonbeams' concert had been a lot of fun. But her adventures in the Rainbow Realm had also left her feeling ready to go home, sit down at her desk, and tackle her math homework. She wanted to see her father and Corey. And, as her stomach grumbled, she realized she was ready for dinner—and especially ready for the lasagna her father had been cooking.

Cressida turned and looked at the unicorn princesses. "I have had such a good time with you today. It was amazing to be the Moonbeams' special guest. But I think it's time for me to go home," she said.

Sunbeam nodded. "Thank you so very much for coming, Cressida."

"Yes," Moon said, "and thank you so much for saving the Moonbeams' concert."

"It was my pleasure," Cressida said. Then she kneeled down and smiled at the owl chicks, who were yawning again. She bet that in a matter of minutes, they would be napping in their strollers. "Goodbye, Oliver, Owen, Orion, Odetta, Olivia, and Orly," she said, grinning at them.

"Goodbye! Goodbye!" the owl chicks called out.

Opal and Otto smiled at Cressida. "It was great to meet you," Opal said.

"Yes, it sure was," Otto said.

"It was wonderful to meet you, too," Cressida said.

She looked again at her friends, the unicorn princesses. "Goodbye!" she sang out, and she held up her jazz hands on either side of her face.

The unicorns princesses laughed.

"Come back soon!" Sunbeam sang out.

"You're always welcome here!" Moon sang.

Bloom and Prism grinned and nodded.

Breeze and Firefly winked.

And Flash and Feather, in their

enthusiastic, off-key voices, belted out, "Goodbye, Cressida!"

Cressida giggled as she pulled her key from her jeans pocket. She pressed the crystal-ball handle between her palms and closed her eyes. "Take me home, please," she said.

The Glitter Canyon began to spin, until all she could see was a blur of sparkling purple. Then, everything went pitch black. Cressida felt herself flying up into the air and soaring through space until she landed on something that felt soft and spongy, like moss. For a few seconds, all she could see was a swirl of blue sky, green leaves, and brown branches. But soon, the woods stopped spinning, and she found herself sitting on a green, mossy patch right beneath the giant oak tree.

She felt her pockets. The microphone and the magic glasses were gone. But there was something else there. Grinning, Cressida pulled out a yellow and black ticket. She stuffed it back in her pocket for safe keeping, stood up, and skipped home, her silver unicorn sneakers blinking all the way.

DON'T MISS OUR NEXT MAGICAL ADVENTURE!

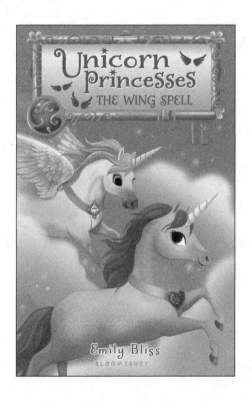

TURN THE PAGE FOR A SNEAK PEEK . . .

Chapter One

In the top tower of Spiral Palace, Ernest, a wizard-lizard, lay in bed under a puffy purple comforter. He stretched and blinked as sunlight streamed through his window. He yawned and rubbed his eyes. And then, with his green scaly hands, he reached over to his bedside table and grabbed a book. In red script across the cover, the title read, *Get It Right the First Time: Ten Easy Tips to End Magical Mishaps and Cast Spells with Confidence.*

Ernest flipped the book open to where he'd left a bookmark. He began to read silently from page 38:

TIP FOUR: Read spells while you're casting them, even if you're completely sure you have them memorized!

Many wizard-lizards insist on trying to memorize spells before they cast them. But attempting to memorize a spell instead of reading it is a leading cause of mistakes. We strongly suggest you read directly from your books while you're casting spells, especially if your spells often result in magical mishaps.

"Hmm," Ernest said to himself. "I don't know about that. I suppose it's worth considering. Maybe."

Before he could continue reading, there was a knock on the door. "Come in," he called.

The door creaked open, and in walked a silver unicorn. Around her neck hung a pink ribbon necklace with a diamond gemstone.

"Princess Flash!" Ernest said, smiling.

Flash looked at Ernest, still lying in bed. "Did I wake you?" she asked.

"Not at all," Ernest said. "I was reading."

"What are you reading?" Flash asked.

"Um, nothing really. Just a book about casting spells," Ernest said, shutting the book and shoving it under his pillow. He slid out from under his comforter and stood, revealing purple-and-white-striped pajamas. "Might I help you with something?" he asked, looking hopeful. "You don't happen to need any magical assistance, do you?"

Emily Bliss lives just down the street from a forest. From her living room window, she can see a big oak tree with a magic keyhole. Like Cressida Jenkins, she knows that unicorns are real.

Sydney Hanson was raised in Minnesota alongside numerous pets and brothers. In addition to her traditional illustrations, Sydney is an experienced 2D and 3D production artist and has worked for several animation shops, including Nickelodeon and Disney Interactive. In her spare time, she enjoys traveling and spending time outside with her adopted brother, a Labrador retriever named Cash. She lives in Los Angeles.

www.sydwiki.tumblr.com